cornbread & poppy

at the museum

matthew cordell

L B

Little, Brown and Company
New York Boston

To Mary-Kate Gaudet—
a friend of Old Larry and a friend of mine

About This Book

The illustrations for this book were done in pen and ink with watercolor. This book was edited by Mary-Kate Gaudet and designed by Angelie Yap. The series is designed by Joann Hill. The production was supervised by Kimberly Stella, and the production editor was Marisa Finkelstein. The text was set in New Century Schoolbook, and the display type is hand lettered.

Contents

The Moonville Museum

One crisp, clear winter's day, an exciting letter arrived. It was a special invitation for Cornbread, plus one guest of his choosing.

Moonville Museum
to the
Esteemed Cornbread

. . . .

You and one guest are hereby
invited to our first Founders Gala—
a special celebration for museum
patrons where a surprise new
exhibit will be revealed.

This Saturday at 2 p.m.
Gourmet cheeses, nuts, and
juices will be served.
Fancy attire is required.

Bagoo! Bagoo!

Cornbread loved the Moonville Museum and all its fascinating artifacts.

The *Toothbrushes Through Time* exhibit…

…the *Molds and Fungi* collection…

...the insect specimens...

...the antique

cheese graters...

...the mummified peanut...

Cornbread loved it all.

But his absolute favorite item at the museum was the priceless, most delicate, perfumed (it smelled like flowers), porcelain Vase of Bagoo.

This prized piece was once owned by the Moonville Museum founder, Ms. Agatha Twicksby Moses Bagoo.

Cornbread put
on his finest
tweed suit.

He brushed his teeth
sparkling white.

Cornbread cleaned up nice!

Then he left his house with plenty of time to
pick up his guest. Naturally, he had invited
his best friend, Poppy.

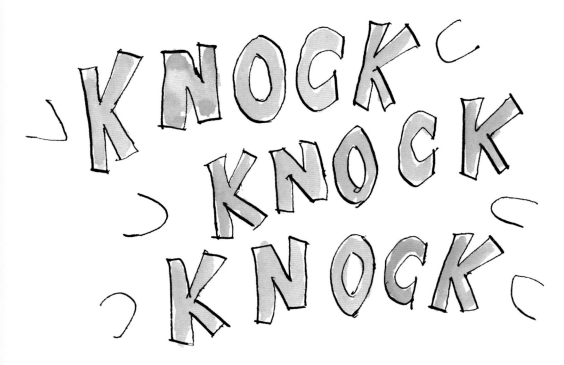

Poppy answered the door, still in her everyday jumpsuit.

"Poppy! You're not ready yet?!" exclaimed Cornbread.

Poppy sighed. "Do I really have to go to this stuffy old thing, Cornbread?"

It was no secret that Poppy had never been interested in the Moonville Museum. Cornbread often invited her, but Poppy never wanted to go. Poppy preferred the outdoors— riding her bike, hiking, and swimming.

Poppy loved adventure.

Spending the day indoors looking at objects did not sound fun to her.

"Poppy, you will love it," Cornbread promised. "I will show you all my favorite things."

"Well...," said Poppy, not quite sure.

"It's the first Founders Gala, so you never know what could happen!"

"Well...," said Poppy, almost convinced.

"And if you don't like it," said Cornbread, "I promise to go camping with you."

Poppy loved the woods as much as
Cornbread loved the museum.

But she could never get him to go camping
with her because he was too afraid.

"Deal!" said Poppy.

Poppy put on her glamorous
dress with sparkles.

She cleaned her
great-great-auntie
Twick's fancy hat and
adjusted it on her head.

Poppy cleaned up nice!

"Okay, Cornbread. Let's go."

❊ The Founders Gala ❊

It was a bustling scene at the Moonville Museum. Cornbread was delighted to see that many of his regular museum friends had shown up in their finest outfits for the gala.

"Hi, Cornbread! Bagoo! Bagoo!" said Grandpa
Bilkins and Tip.

"Bagoo! Bagoo!" responded Cornbread. "Our
greeting in honor of the founder," he explained
to Poppy.

"Cornbread, old bean! Bagoo! Bagoo!"
exclaimed Templeton and Jericho.

"Nice to see you again, Cornbread!

Bagoo! Bagoo!" said Carroll and Frostburger.

Even grumpy Old Larry had come to the gala.

"I'm just here to tell everybody not to touch
the stuff. Hands off!" he shouted.

27

As everyone had snacks and waited for the big announcement, Cornbread took this time to show Poppy some of his favorite things about the museum.

The *Toothbrushes Through Time*!

"Um…that's *interesting*, Cornbread," said Poppy unconvincingly.

The *Molds and Fungi*!

"Something smells...*not good* in here,
Cornbread," said Poppy uncomfortably.

The insect specimens!

"This is a little…*creepy*," said Poppy, less than enthused.

31

Cornbread was disappointed in Poppy's
reaction. He wanted her to like the Moonville
Museum as much as he did.

But Poppy would surely be impressed by the
priceless, most delicate, perfumed (it smelled
like flowers), porcelain Vase of Bagoo.

Just then, a voice came over a loudspeaker. It was the museum director, Prudence Farnsworth.

"Bagoo! Bagoo! Gather round, everyone, for the unveiling of our latest exhibit!"

At the count of three, a large red velvet curtain opened up, revealing a room of spectacular treasures.

The Bagoo Collection

"The Bagoo Collection!"

The surprise new exhibit! An entire gallery devoted to the personal collection of Ms. Agatha Twicksby Moses Bagoo.

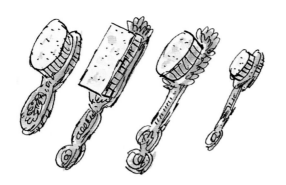

Her hand-carved hairbrushes.

Her diamond-encrusted perfume sprayers.

Her solid-gold ice-cream scoop.

And more!

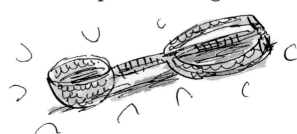

Prominently displayed at
the center of the collection
was a never-before-seen
portrait of the Moonville
Museum founder herself,
Ms. Agatha Twicksby
Moses Bagoo.

Everyone *ooh*ed!

Everyone *aah*ed!

Everyone except for Poppy, who took one look around, then stood at the portrait and said, "This stuff is just too fancy for me!"

Everyone gasped!

GASSSP!!

Because when they looked at Poppy...

…and they looked at the portrait…

"The resemblance is uncanny!" said Prudence
Farnsworth.

Poppy looked *just like* Agatha Twicksby Moses
Bagoo! *All* the way up to her great-great-auntie
Twick's hat!

Everyone gathered around Poppy.

Cornbread was pushed to the side.

Prudence Farnsworth consulted the town records. Great-Great-Auntie Twick was the youngest third-generation niece of Ms. Agatha Twicksby Moses Bagoo.

Which meant...

…Poppy was related to the Bagoos!

Suddenly, everyone at the museum was interested in Poppy.

And suddenly, no one at the museum was interested in Cornbread.

Cornbread walked away, sad and sniffling, with tears in his eyes and his head held low.

Sniff sniff.

It smelled like flowers.

"CORNBREAD, WATCH OUT!"

yelled Poppy.

But before he could even look up, it was too late.

The Vase of Bagoo

Cornbread collided with his favorite museum object! The priceless, most delicate, perfumed (it smelled like flowers), porcelain Vase of Bagoo tipped over and shattered on the museum floor.

54

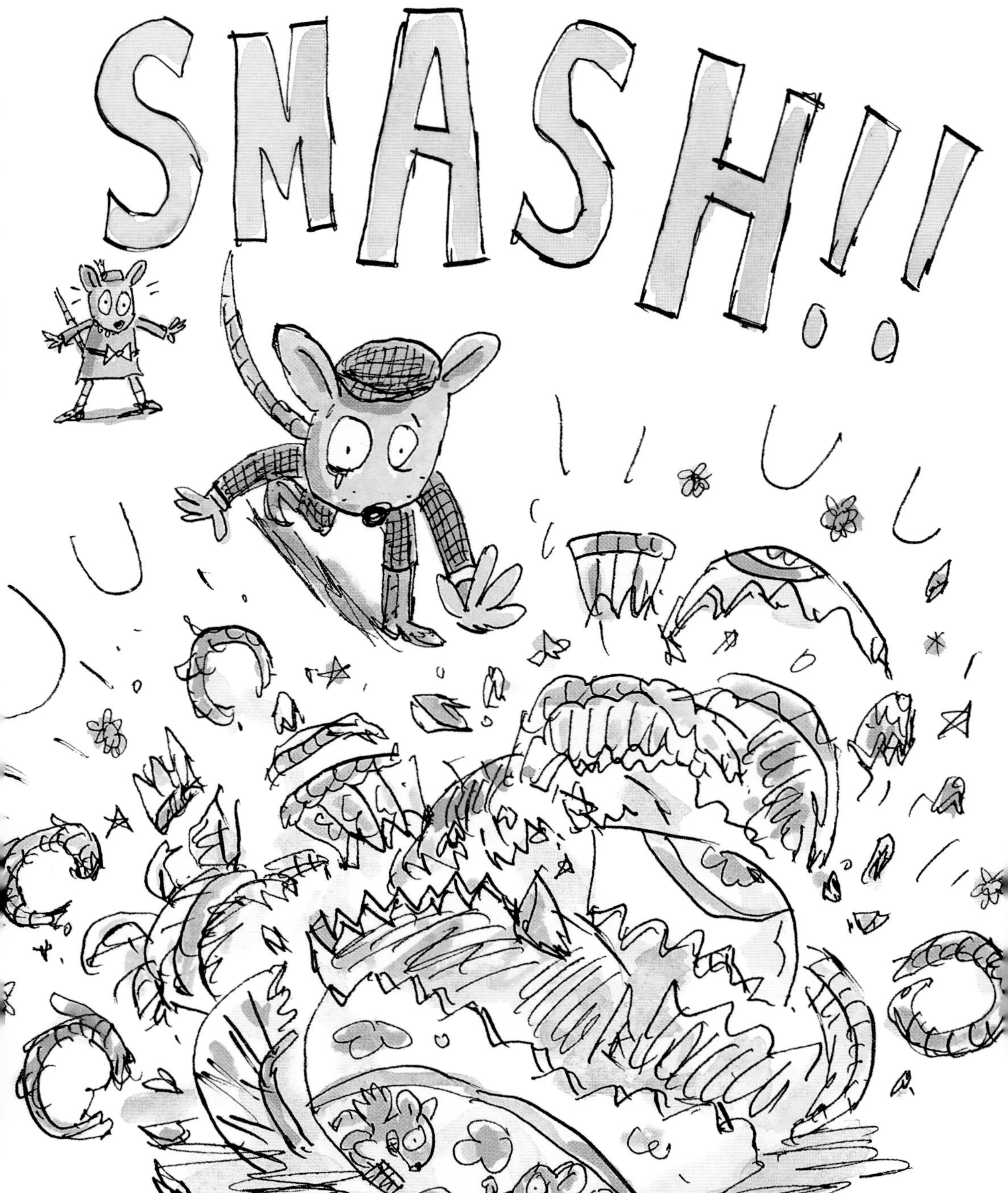
SMASH!!

Everyone shrieked!

Poppy ran over to help her friend.

"Cornbread, what in the world was that?" she asked.

"This, Poppy, was everyone's favorite object at the museum. It's what's left of the irreplaceable Vase of Bagoo! I'll never be able to show my face here again. The Founders Gala has been a complete disaster," sobbed Cornbread.

61

Poppy looked closely at the shards on the floor.
She sniffed at the floral scent.

SNIFF
SNIFF

"I can help," she said. "I have a vase just like
this one that's been in my family for years.
It smells so much I keep it in the attic!"

Cornbread swept up the pieces, and they went
to fetch the replacement vase.

"Here it is," said Poppy, holding her nose.

"Here it is!" said Cornbread, sniffing in deep.

"I was maybe a little jealous back there, Poppy.

"I think it's amazing that you're a Bagoo!" said Cornbread.

"Thanks, Cornbread," said Poppy.

"But maybe we can talk after we get this thing to the museum?"

"Thank you," said Cornbread. "You're a good friend, Poppy."

"The priceless, most delicate, perfumed (it smells like flowers), porcelain Vase of Bagoo! Part two!" shouted Prudence Farnsworth.

"Huzzah!" everyone cheered.

"I really wanted you to like the museum as much as I do, Poppy." Cornbread sighed.

"You know...," said Poppy. "I did like it! It *was* an adventure. I even learned something about my family. Bagoo! Bagoo!"

"Bagoo! Bagoo!" said Cornbread.

"And I got to spend the day with you," said Poppy. "You're a good friend, Cornbread."

"Great! We'll go every week!" exclaimed Cornbread.

"For you," said Poppy, "I will go *sometimes*. As long as I don't have to wear this dusty old hat," said Poppy.

"Deal!" said Cornbread.

"And as long as you go camping with me next week," said Poppy.

"Well...," said Cornbread.